Metaphorosis

February 2019

Beautifully made speculative fiction

Also from Metaphorosis Books

Score – an SFF symphony

Reading 5X5: Readers' Edition
Reading 5X5: Writers' Edition

Best Vegan Science Fiction & Fantasy

Best Vegan SFF of 2018
Best Vegan SFF of 2017
Best Vegan SFF of 2016

Metaphorosis Magazine

Metaphorosis: Best of 2018
Metaphorosis: Best of 2017
Metaphorosis: Best of 2016

Metaphorosis 2018: The Complete Stories
Metaphorosis 2017: The Complete Stories
Metaphorosis 2016: Nearly Complete Stories

Monthly issues

by B. Morris Allen

Susurrus
Allenthology: Volume I
Tocsin: and other stories
Start with Stones: collected stories
Metaphorosis: a collection of stories

Metaphorosis

February 2019

edited by
B. Morris Allen

Metaphorosis Books

Neskowin

ISSN: 2573-136X (online)
ISBN: 978-1-64076-133-9 (e-book)
ISBN: 978-1-64076-134-6 (paperback)

February 2019

The Lightkeeper's Wife

Amelia Dee Mueller

The first time Elsie Frasier tried to murder her husband, the other women of Auskerry called it a pretty meager attempt. Some insisted it might even have been an accident. He had fallen down the last flight of stairs in the couple's lighthouse and only fractured the smaller bone in his arm.

The next time, when he fell from his ladder while painting the kitchen cupboards, was nearly two years later, much too long when compared to Claire McKinney, who held the record at sixteen attempts in six months alone. She only had to spend one year and three months on the island before she successfully murdered Mr. McKinney, found her stolen seal skin, and returned to the sea.

That Monday, when Elsie went to town to pick up her groceries, the other selkies surrounded her in the street. They were led by Elspeth Donoghue. Elspeth was an old woman, gray and wrinkled, with a middle that swayed as she walked, and she leaned on a cane to accommodate her hunch. She had yet to rid herself of the even older and even more hunched Mr. Donaghue, but it wasn't for lack of trying.

"Good morning, Mrs. Frasier," Elspeth said, cutting Elsie off as she stepped into Auskerry's single road.

Elsie smiled, but her fingers twitched as she offered her hand to shake. She was desperate the avoid the selkies most days, though she didn't judge their violent traditions. She also hated the men who snatched them from the sea, but she liked to stay out of the way. She saw fewer selkies on the island these days anyway. Men with selkie brides always found good fortune, but the world was changing. The young men of Auskerry were more likely to leave the island to find their fortune than risk capturing a selkie bride and getting murdered afterward.

Elsie hoped the evolving world of 1920 proved that this tradition was dying, which would mean the other selkies might stop questioning her marriage. But when Elspeth wouldn't take her outstretched hand, Elsie knew that this wasn't to be.

"We just came to say, my dear, that we're worried about you," Elspeth said. "Nearly four years you've been married, and only two attempts to rid yourself of this form! Is your husband making it particularly difficult for you? Is he clever? It's rare for a human man, but I've seen it all, dearie."

Elsie squared her shoulders. "I have it under control."

As she turned away, Elspeth's cane struck out against a store's brick front, trapping Elsie. Other women stopped to watch, but they were mostly the daughters or granddaughters of selkies. Though every year less and less of the Auskerry men risked marrying selkies, it was still true that the richest men on the island all had pure selkie wives, and that they all retired fat, lived lavishly, and died young.

It was difficult to marry a selkie. First, a man had to trap one, and then drag her back to the mainland without being drowned, and then succeed at ripping away her seal skin to reveal the human form beneath. The wedding was done before the selkie had her wits back, and by then the man would have hidden her skin away in an expert hiding spot. By the time the selkie was aware of her situation, her skin was gone, and she would spend the rest of her human life trying to kill the man who took it from her.

"We don't think you do, lass," Elspeth said, wagging one of her fat, sausage fingers. "Is it true he hasn't even hidden your skin from you?"

The selkies gasped. There was only a handful of them, a sharp contrast to the hundreds that must have walked the island in Elspeth's youth. Few were young, and they stood with their hands folded and lips pursed. The young ones still wore their hair loose in long curls that blew in the wind. They remembered the sea with a fresher pain, having been plucked out only recently, and the fierceness with which they shoved their husbands off ladders or down wells was like a storm breaking on a cliff.

The rest were middle aged and wore their hair in strict plaits down their backs, leaving their pinched faces and creased foreheads exposed. They were so square and stiff that it was obvious that they barely remembered what it was like to be weightless in the water, and every time they swung a pot against the back of their husbands' heads, their swings grew wearier and wearier. Just a spring gale trying to topple a sail boat.

Elspeth was the oldest. Elsie had heard stories of kidnapped selkies stranded on land and forced to die human deaths, but as a young pup she had never thought that she would actually meet one. Even if Elspeth managed to retrieve her skin, there was no guarantee it would still fit her. Her dress stuck to the rolls around her middle like a sausage casing about to rip.

"It's unnatural, it is," Elspeth said. "Wanting what you got. My generation fought to protect yours, killing as many of these men as we did. You're putting all our hard work to shame. Making it into nothing. How can you disrespect your own kind like that?"

The selkies behind her muttered their agreement. They looked at Elsie with loathing. They couldn't comprehend how a selkie with access to her skin would choose to stay on land, and they hated her for it. Their envy was ripe on their pinched faces, and Elsie could taste it on the wind.

"I had a choice," Elsie said, still calm, still trying to make them understand. "What I have is nothing like what you were forced into."

Elspeth spit at her feet, rubbing it into the street with the end of her cane. "You only think you did! They're all the same, lass. Even the ones trying to hide it. And we gotta protect our own, especially when she can't see two feet in in front of her own face."

Elsie hiked her shopping basket onto her shoulder and turned away from the group. She heard them whispering behind her, but she didn't look back.

"We'll be checking in soon!" Elspeth called. "To lend you a hand!"

Outside the village, the road tapered off into the overgrown path that led to the Auskerry Lighthouse. The tower of the lighthouse, at only eighty-six feet, was fatter and shorter than the others along the Scottish coast, and was mostly white but for the candy stripe of red across its middle.

The Frasiers lived in the small house at its base. Its paint was always peeling from the salty winds and the front door never hung straight. The windows creaked during storms, and its two small rooms were packed with heirloom quilts and furniture, and stuffed with colorful knickknacks, and layered with wall hangings and pictures that hung lopsided.

Elsie heard a curse from the shed that held the lamp oil, and she was knocked back a few steps by the scent of kerosene as she approached.

Tom was covered in it. He dripped it onto the grass as he came out, and flicked it onto her skirts as he shook out his legs.

"We've got too much of this stuff now that we switched to Hood's damned invention!" he said, wiping his face with his oil-soaked shirt. "I can't walk in there without knocking it over!"

"Why do you keep ordering the same amount?" Elsie asked, her face turned away from the wind so the smell wouldn't reach her. They had installed the new lamp a year ago at the insistence of the Northern Lighthouse Board, as it required less oil but burned brighter, but Tom had not stopped complaining.

"You never know with these new contraptions," he said. "What would happen if we ran out? Ships lining up to crash, debris raining down from the sea, bodies along the beach. I don't like to take chances."

Tom's family had run he lighthouse at Stronsay Firth since it'd been built in 1889, and the farthest he'd ever been from it was the night his father died. The trembling teenager had barely laid his father's cold, limp hand back onto the blankets of his deathbed before his mother got to tearing the lighthouse apart. She went through every cupboard and trunk, ripped down all the curtains, dug up the garden, tore up the floorboards, and found her stolen skin rolled into a ball and stuffed in the toilet tank. Tom watched from the window as she went to the cliff, wrapped the skin around herself, and leapt headfirst into the rolling white sea below.

Tom chased after her, knowing it was a hopeless risk. A selkie had never been found again after escaping, but he went anyway, terrified to think of living alone in the bleak, empty lighthouse. He climbed down the crags of the cliffs, clutching to the rocks as the hard island winds tried to tear him from the edge, and set out for the open sea in his father's boat. Tom didn't find his mother, and he realized too late that the lamp in the lighthouse had not been lit, and he was drifting out to open sea with nothing to guide him back.

Elsie first saw him bobbing in the waves like a message in a bottle. She, like the other women of her kind, was wary of the human men who hunted her. Any man who made his living by the sea benefited from the good fortune a selkie wife would bring. Selkie women spent their entire lives not getting too close, but Elsie drifted toward the tiny boat. This human looked sad, with his head in his hands on the dark sea, and she took pity on him. She grabbed a piece of rope and towed him back to the island.

When they reached land, she stayed in the shallows, watching him drag the boat back to shore, nudging it firmly in the wet sand. He looked back at her and gave a sheepish wave as thanks, and she found herself swimming closer. As she approached the beach, the soft folds of her skin shed, falling around her legs like a robe. She knew stories of selkies plucked from the sea, their skins shorn from their naked forms with gutting knives, left at the bottom of the hunters' boats until they were forced to walk on awkward, unwanted legs. But this felt different. Walking was natural, like breathing.

She gathered up her skin as she stepped onto the beach, the tiny grains of sand squishing between her toes for the first time, the breeze tickling her skin and whipping her long, wet curls. She looked at Tom, and his face was as red as a sunset the night before a storm. He shrugged off his coat and offered it her. Elsie followed him into the lighthouse, and she never returned to the sea.

"I'm going to wash up," Tom said now, starting for the house. Elsie maneuvered in front of him.

"Go to the beach or sleep in the tower," she said. "I won't have kerosene stinking up my house."

"My own wife banishing me to the sea!" Tom said, but he was grinning. "At least let me take a kiss with me when I turn to ice and sink to the bottom."

She side-stepped his outstretched arms, but he caught her around the waist and his greasy, oil-soaked lips kissed her cheek. Any other day she would've laughed, but the oil was cold and it sent shivers down her spine, and she couldn't get the image of Elspeth's fat fingers pointing at her out of her head. Tom stepped back as she wiped the slime from her face.

"What's wrong?" he said.

"Get cleaned up. I'll tell you when you get back."

He frowned, but he wandered off down the cliff-side path that led to the beach.

Elsie went to the house and twisted the kitchen light switch on. She was still getting used to the foreign, artificial glow that electricity made. She much preferred the heartbeat of a gas light. It was the lighthouse's pulsing, steady light that had drawn her near the shores of Auskerry in the first place. All selkies were drawn by a lighthouse's lamp, entranced by its glow and swinging beam, though they knew it could be the end of their freedom. Elsie remembered as a young pup promising to never get too close to the low, yellow star on the horizon, no matter how beautiful it might seem. It was a promise few selkies could keep.

Elsie put the groceries away in the cupboards, leaving out a few of the smaller potatoes for dinner, and hung her basket on the back of the bedroom door. She stood in the doorway, hesitating before turning that light on.

Under the bed was a package wrapped in a thick, woolen blanket and tied with rope. Elsie slid it into her lap. It was in a tight, expert knot, and her fingers were raw by the time she had it undone. Inside were sheets of neat white paper, and Elsie peeled them back one by one, careful not to crease any, until she'd reached the brown skin beneath. It crinkled as she lifted it. The once soft hide was stiff and rough with dried salt. She laid it out flat on the bedroom floor, tracing the edge with her fingertip, realizing that it was smaller than she remembered.

She heard Tom at the door. He leaned against the frame, drying his face with a dishcloth.

"You're not going to leave me, are you?" he said, grinning. He wrung the water out of the cloth with a tight squeeze and threw it over his shoulder.

"Never," she said and folded it back inside the blanket.

"What's bothering you?" He sat on the edge of the bed, leaning over his knees. "What happened?"

She told him about her conversation with Elspeth in the village, and he laughed.

"That old hag," he said, slapping the cloth across his knee. "How long has she been trying to knock off poor Donoghue? Fifty years? Isn't she satisfied with one man to murder?"

Elsie sat on the bed beside him. "She says I'm betraying my own kind. All the others were with her."

Tom was silent. He clasped his hands in front of him. "Do you agree?"

Elsie clenched her fists. "I chose you. It's not the same. But they don't understand. They think all the humans are awful, and can't comprehend how a selkie could be happy with one." She clenched her fists. "They're not even trying to understand."

She wanted to rip something apart. For years she'd taken the passive glares from the other selkies, and had carefully avoided running into them in the village. As long as she and Tom didn't interfere with the way of things, Elsie had thought they could get along. The selkies were letting their jealousy, and their superiority, make life-threatening assumptions. No selkie could possibly want to be chained to a man's side, they said. And they were right. No selkie could want that, but one might choose to stand at his side on her own two legs. But Elsie wasn't sure she could ever make them understand this.

"How about you knock a vase over my head?" Tom suggested. "We'll show them the glass, and I'll walk around the village with a bandaged forehead for a few days."

"This isn't like before," Elsie said. "You can't fake it again. We need to leave."

He leaned back, his arm hanging off the end of the bedframe. "And go where?"

"Anywhere—the mainland, another island. We can't stay here, Tom. They want to kill you."

"We're not leaving Auskerry." He threw the cloth at his feet. His jaw was tight and fists clenched as he went to stand at the end of the bed. "Who would tend the light? Do you know what would happen if that went out?" He pointed above his head. "Everyone would die. Sailors, fishermen, the entire damn village. We live by that light."

"You can't tend to the lamp if you're dead!" Elsie cried, leaping up as he began to pace.

"We can't abandon it," he said. He wouldn't look at her. "We're not leaving."

He left and she heard him rummaging through a cupboard. He was going to light the lamp, like he did every night, and Elsie waited until she heard the front door slam shut before going back to the kitchen. He would be up there until dinner time, and return for the first few hours of the night, just to keep an eye on things. This was Tom's pattern, copied from his father's days as lightkeeper.

Elsie mashed the potatoes, pairing them with the vegetables she'd just bought, and putting it on their chipped plates. She waited thirty minutes, then an hour, then two, before she threw both untouched meals in the sink, spattering potatoes on the counter. She went outside and looked up at the tower and saw her husband's silhouette at its top. She went inside and turned the lights off without washing up.

Elsie twisted in bed until Tom came down, but she feigned sleep until she heard his breathing settle. She slid out from beneath their warm woolen blanket and went to the kitchen, putting on a kettle to boil. She shivered in the harsh, evening air. She could hear Tom start to snore softly in the bedroom, and she shook her head as she poured boiled water into her cup. She wanted to hate him for his stubborn resilience, but she was glad of it. She was like the

sea—whirling and wondering and guessing which way the currents would pull them next, and he was the land. Firm and set, with roots too deep to pull. Their love met somewhere on the shore, a balancing act of pushing and pulling the sand and the water into different directions. He would never leave his lighthouse, and she would never leave him. She would think of a different way.

She turned from the stove and lifted the cup to her lips, thinking she might go up to the tower to drink it. She opened the front door, and the cup slid from her hands and shattered on the kitchen floor.

A haggard, wrinkled face stood in her doorway, cast in harsh shadows as the beam of the lighthouse swung around behind it. Elspeth leaned on her cane with one hand and held a fisherman's gutting knife in the other. The wind whipped her greasy grey hair across her face, and behind her the beam of the lighthouse swung across the island's path. In its light

Elsie saw a crowd of selkies. They held kitchen knives and pitchforks and frying pans, but the second the light was gone, they disappeared into shadow.

Elsie slammed the door in Elspeth's face. She stood frozen in her kitchen, cold beads of sweat soaking her nightgown. She waited for them to rip her door down. She pictured them tearing into her bedroom and lifting Tom from his bed. She imagined his scream as they stuck their knives in him, and she thought of Elspeth's grin as her knife ripped through the flesh at his throat.

"Elsie?" Tom said from their bedroom doorway, calling her back from her imaginings. He rubbed sleep from his eyes. "What are you doing?"

Elsie crept toward their window to peer out into the dark. But the selkies had gone.

"Nothing," she said. Her jaw tightened. "I was doing nothing."

Elsie did not sleep that night, but she was up with Tom just after sunrise to make breakfast and to help carry kerosene up the lighthouse steps. She stayed by his side during the day, wiping away soot from the huge prisms of the Fresnel lens that circled the flame. She helped him to rewind the clockwork that turned the lamp, and to lock the weights into place. She watched him trim the wicks and close the curtains of the lantern room to protect the lens from discoloration.

A thick fog came during the afternoon, and they rushed to light the lamp. She waited with him on the gallery to watch for passing ships. Beyond was only sea on one side, and a dirty, barely green island on the other, where the village stood far below like a toy that Elsie could lift her boot above and smash. She thought she could pick out Elspeth's house, larger than all the rest, with neat tiles set out in perfect rows and a well-manicured garden. She spat at that house, but the wind carried the spittle away.

There hadn't been a crash on Auskerry since Elsie had arrived, but Tom had told her of one from his childhood. It had been a great steel steamer, too large to turn in time, chugging through icy waters at night during a storm. Everyone had been asleep but for Tom's father, who watched helplessly as the ship met its end and heard the long groan of the steel cutting against the rocks that lined the firth.

Elsie had forgotten about that ship until he'd told the story. She'd been there, safe beneath the waves while the storm raged far above. She and the other selkies watched as it cut into rock. They'd felt the vibrations of crunching metal shudder through the water, and seen the bodies falling into the waves. The selkies curled their lips, showing their yellowed, pointed teeth, as they swam toward the flailing limbs of the sailors. One by one, the selkies snatched them and dragged them beneath the surface until they stopped kicking. Elsie and the other pups had been meant to watch and learn. The selkies were shrinking the human numbers, slowly but surely, the elders said, and soon there would be no more selkies torn from their families. Elsie had been the first to look away.

Wreckage and bodies washed up on the shore for weeks, and the huge engine could still be seen at low tide at just the right angle from the cliff. It reminded Elsie of a great sea creature, stretching its gaping mouth out of the water, desperate for air.

Tom went to sit on the tower steps, wiping the oil and grit from his hands. Elsie took the step just below his, hugging herself. He looked down at her.

"Thank you," he said, placing a hand on her shoulder.

"For what?"

He drew her against him. "For not asking me to leave again."

Elsie laid her head in her hands, but she saw Elspeth's sunken eyes looking back. She pulled away from her husband and stood up, looking out at the rolling fog and listening to the waves far below it. If she could spare Tom the pain of leaving his lighthouse, she would. No matter the cost to herself, or to her kind. What had they ever done for her?

"Can I ask you for something else?" she said.

"I don't like the sound of that," Tom said.

Elsie didn't like the thought of it. She wasn't sure she would have the time to pull it off, or if it would work. She wondered if the Auskerry selkies would kill her, and Tom with her, if she succeeded, but she knew that they would take him from her if she failed. She could imagine them wrapping her in her dried skin, feeling its papery touch, and then the slip of her transformation as they dropped her in the ocean. There was part of her that wanted to feel the stream of the water, to push through its currents and waves and swim down farther and farther into the darkness to the cold depths. But that part was dull and lifeless compared to the race and warmth of her heart as she looked at Tom.

If she managed it all, they could be left to enjoy their human lives together, without humans or selkies. There might be unavoidable casualties, she knew, but both species had brought it upon themselves.

"Tomorrow night, can we not light the lamp?"

He put a hand to his heart as if she had stabbed him. "Why?"

"I can't tell you. Not yet. It's just one night, Tom."

"One night can mean life and death to one ship."

"Please," she said. "There's only way I can think of to keep us here."

Tom leaned away from her, one hand rubbing the back of his neck. "Let me think on it."

That night there was a storm. Tom pulled a raincoat on over his keeper's uniform after dinner and sat at the dining room table lacing up his boots.

"I'll be up all night," he said. "It's supposed to be bad, and the lamp will need constant tending. You'll be all right on your own?"

"Just be careful," Elsie said, drying the last dish and putting it away.

"You come up if you get lonely," he said, and kissed her on the cheek.

She heard him open the door to the tower, and the faint thud of his footsteps on the iron staircase. He'd stop to check the weights before he went to the service room. He'd sit on the same stool in front of the same window, the one with the clearest view, and he'd watch the beam swing back and forth across the sea. He'd only hear the crash of the waves, or the ring of the thunder. Elsie sat on the edge of her bed to lace up her boots.

The rain beat against her window, slipping down the glass in thick streaks. There was no going back after this. She tried to feel hesitant. Maybe she could do something less drastic. They were, after all, her kind. And their actions were defensible. To have their freedom ripped away and hidden was a jarring, unforgivable crime. They were forced to live a foreign life. Elsie watched the water slip down the window and thought of her husband and of Elspeth's words, and she felt the same helplessness she knew the selkies must feel. It enraged her that they were the cause of it. They were her kind; how could they push their fears on her with their threats? They were the cause of her helplessness, just as the humans were the cause of theirs.

Elsie looked one last time for guilt and hesitation, but it didn't come. She stood up and pulled on her raincoat.

It was the kind of storm with rain that fell anywhere but down. It hit her face horizontally like icy pellets, or splashed up from puddles on the ground into her boots and soaked her stockings. Her coat didn't do much good, and she let the hood fall while she went to the storage shed. The kerosene was against the wall in steel cans painted green with a spout on one side and a curved, rusted handle on the other. In the corner, Elsie found a wooden cart to carry them in.

Only four cans would fit in the cart. She started off down the road to the village by pulling it, but she realized that she'd have to push it over the larger bumps and dips. The cans were heavy, and they knocked and banged together, their liquid slurring inside.

There were only a few flickering candles in the windows of the village houses. The rain dripped rhythmically onto the rooftops, and the water pooled in the street. There was a mixed scent of fresh and salt water, but it was soon overpowered by the kerosene.

Elsie started at Elspeth's house. She lined her walls with two cans worth before moving on to her neighbors. She liked the sound of the kerosene sloshing out of the can and splattering the houses. She threw the last can back in the cart and dug her matches out of her pocket, careful to keep them under her coat and out of the rain. But they were already wet.

"Damn," she muttered, throwing them away. She didn't have time to go back to the house.

The Donoghue's door wasn't locked. Elsie let herself in, not bothering to shut it behind her. The front door led into the kitchen, and she found the matches in the drawer next to the candles. She took them into the bedroom.

The Donoghue's were misshapen lumps on the bed. Their blanket didn't quit cover their legs, and they stuck out like veiny, swollen tongues. Elsie lit a match and held it against the corner of their blanket until it took. She waited until the smoke hung thick and black in the air before slipping back out.

She threw a few more matches against the houses as she went, and left the rest on the road. The heat didn't really start to rise until she was out of sight of the village, and it wasn't until she heard people shouting that she turned around to look.

The bright orange and yellow against the dark sky was jarring. She'd never seen anything so bright in all her life. It overwhelmed the sky, swallowing the stars and spitting up smoke. The rain had begun to lighten, but lightning still split across the darkness, right above the flames. It blinded her. She tried to imagine what the light would look like beneath the ocean, but she couldn't picture it.

At the house, Elsie dragged the cart behind her down the rocky path that led to the cliff. She tossed her cans in one at a time, and in between the flashes of lightning she could see bright yellow eyes looking back at her. There were hundreds of pairs, luminescent against the black water, bobbing with the roll and sway of the storm. They didn't see her, but the flickering arches of flames were reflected in their yellow eyes. The selkies were entranced by the burning of the village of Auskerry, and Elsie hoped the light would keep them fixated until morning, so they would stay close to the shores during the day, and let her handle them that next night.

The morning, Tom insisted they go help at the village, and Elsie followed silently behind him. Most of the structures in Auskerry were made of wood, and all that was left that morning were their blackened carcasses. A few of the stone shops had survived, though their glass windows had cracked.

"Was anyone hurt?" Tom asked Mr. McDougal, a shopkeeper, as he helped him haul away what was left of his house.

"Just old Donoghue and his wife. Rest of us got a fair warning, but they never rose from their beds. Think it was the smoke," McDougal said.

"What happened?"

"Lightning strike, we're saying. Who knows? Lots of folks talking about leaving for good—cheaper to start over on the mainland. Try for some factory work."

Most of the selkies were on their hands and knees sorting through wreckage, searching desperately for their charred skins. Elsie leaned against the stone wall of a shop and watched them. They looked up at her a few times, some with jealousy and the older ones with suspicion. She nodded at them, and then went inside to buy a carton of cigarettes.

The cleanup took all day and into the evening. Tom looked toward the horizon as the sun began to sink, and his fingers tightened around the wheelbarrow of debris he pushed. Elsie put a hand on his shoulder.

"Just one night," she said.

"I wish you'd tell me what you're up to."

She let her hand fall. "I don't think you'd like me very much if I did."

He looked down at her, and then back at the charred pieces of village in his wheelbarrow, and his eyes widened. "What have you done?" he said.

"Just something I had to do," she said.

"Did you kill Elspeth and her husband?" he said. "Are you insane?"

"She threatened to kill you," Elsie said. She pursed her lips. "And he kidnapped a selkie. They deserved worse."

Tom dropped the wheelbarrow, toppling it on its side and scattering its contents. He put a hand on Elsie's shoulder and pulled her close. His voice shook as he whispered. "You're a murderer, Elsie. You can't go taking justice into our own hands. It isn't right."

"Whose hands should we take it to, then?" Elsie snapped back. "It was us or them. It was a choice that had to be made."

"Why did it have to be made by you?" he asked.

"It has to end, Tom," Elsie said, glancing around at the selkies and the humans picking through what was left of the village. "And they're not going to do stop it, none of them. Humans will keep kidnapping, and selkies will keep killing. Over and over again until the sea dries out. I've taken care of the humans. Auskerry won't survive if they all leave. Now I have to handle the selkies."

"Maybe you're interfering with what you shouldn't," Tom said, leaning close to her. "Maybe we're not supposed to stop it."

Elsie shook her head. "It's too late for that kind of talk. Whether I'm supposed to or not, I've made up my mind. Give me one night."

"I'm not worth whatever you're planning," he said. "Don't take any more lives because of me."

She could feel the glares of the selkies on her back and remembered the flash of their kitchen knives. She leaned in to kiss her husband.

"I'd do anything for you," she said. "But I won't be killing anyone else. Soon it'll just be the two of us, Tom, safe on our little island. I just need one night."

The lightkeeper put his hands on his hips and slowly nodded.

Elsie burned through three cigarettes on her walk back to the lighthouse, dropping their husks on the path, and lit another as she entered her bedroom. She dragged the package out from beneath the bed and stopped at the shed for another can of kerosene before heading toward the cliff.

It looked out over a rolling green sea painted purple from the dusk. Clouds formed on the horizon, the waves rising and swelling beneath the sky. If she squinted, Elsie could still see bobbing seal shapes along the Auskerry shoreline, resting after a long swim to see the village go up in flame. Elsie dropped the package at her feet and poured the oil over it. It soaked straight through the thin paper, drenching her seal skin beneath.

"You killed Elspeth."

Elsie looked back over her shoulder at Sarah McCreedy, a young selkie who clutched a burnt piece of seal skin to her chest. She stood with four others, all young with wind-swept hair and salty tear streaks and charred skins in their arms. They were the youngest selkies on the island and, if Elsie was successful, the last Auskerry would ever see.

"And now we can never go back," said another that Elsie didn't recognize. "How could you do this to us?"

The guilt Elsie had been looking for last night appeared swiftly, but just as the lightest touch. It made her lip twitch as she turned away from the girls. She liked to believe that they had been brainwashed by Elspeth and the older selkies, but she knew their rage was as strong as hers. They would never forgive what she had done, but she hoped one day when they had lived longer lives and seen harsher things, that they might understand her decision. Even if she had made this choice for all of them, she had not enjoyed it. She would carry it with her, a dull ache that burned as steadily and surely as the lighthouse lamp.

"It had to be done," said Elsie. "By someone."

"We were just trying to help you!" Sarah shouted. "You had no right to take anything from us!"

Elsie spun on her heel, the cigarette flying from her fingertips. "You had no right! You tried to take me from my home, the same way you were taken from yours. How dare you tell me what I should want?"

The selkies cried into the wind, shoulders shaking with their faces in their hands. Elsie turned away and lit a match. She watched the waves bump and roll against the cliff side as she dropped it onto her oil-soaked seal skin. It lit up easily, and she closed her eyes, feeling the sting of the burn deep within her before it settled into a dull warmth. She kicked the package over the cliff.

Sarah wiped her nose with her sleeve. "What are you doing?"

"Giving the humans a chance," Elsie said. "I'll send the selkies away, but they'll be back. By then Auskerry will just be another abandoned rock along the coast with only a lighthouse, just like hundreds of others." She smiled at the thought of their little tower standing tall over the empty island. "And if not, I'll keep burning villages until it is."

"You can't control everything like that," whispered one of the other selkies.

Elsie wasn't listening. She focused on the burning skin. It floated on the water, a beacon of fire against the dark waves, and was pulled out by the current. As it went, the heads of the selkies bobbed up to the surface, following the path of the flames with their bright yellow eyes. They looked back at Elsie, who lit a match and dropped it over the cliff. The selkies watched it fall and vanish into the dark, and then they turned to follow the burning package out into the open ocean and away from the shores of Auskerry.

See Amelia Dee Mueller's story "The Lightkeeper's Wife" online at Metaphorosis. If you liked it, leave a comment. Authors love that!
Remember to subscribe to our e-mail updates so you'll know when new stories are posted.

About the story

I wrote "The Lightkeeper's Wife" for a workshop I took under Blake Kimzey in Dallas. I had nothing to turn in for our second assigned story, so I was brainstorming an idea. I've always been a mythology nerd, and I knew I wanted to write about some kind of mythological creature. I was flipping through a book on famous Scotland myths and found a story mentioning selkies. The female selkies of Scottish lore are described as very demure and submissive, and that just wasn't going to fly for me. I wondered why these women weren't immediately murdering the men who kidnapped them. So, that was my first "what if" moment, which inspired my first line, and the bones of the story fell into place after that.

A question for the author

Q: How   do   pets/children/significant   others help/hinder your process?

A: I keep the part of me that's a writer a bit secluded from my family and friends, and they don't really hear from that part unless I have a piece that's done and ready to be torn apart by the real world. By then I've built some armor around the work and can take any comments they might have, good or bad. If I let people whose opinions I highly value see a piece before it's ready, I wouldn't be able to take any of their criticism, no matter how constructive. Strangers' comments, however, I can take all day long and feel very little personal affiliation and see the room for improvement their negative feedback can bring. I think this comes from my journalism degree, because I didn't have a choice as an undergrad but to let strangers eat up my words and spit them out again. I personally found that my journalism instructors were tougher than the creative writing teachers I worked under for my minor, but they all made me a better writer in the end.

The only thing that might hinder the creative writer in me is my day job, which I love, but it's hard to sit down in the evening to write and mentally switch from the kind of writing I do for work to the kind of writing I do for me.

But my cat generally lets me work in peace, because if I'm writing it means I'm not forcing her to cuddle with me. She, similar to lots of great writers, needs her space.

About the author

Amelia Dee Mueller lives in Dallas and is constantly disappointed that the Old West isn't as present as one would think. A communications coordinator in local government by day, she spends her nights writing, reading, fencing, and streaming superhero movies with her cat. You can follow her on Twitter @AmeliaDMueller.

The Soul Farmer's Daughters

Kyle Kirrin

Thirteen souls flit about in mason jars on the mantle above my workbench. They're bright—luminescent, even—but they're not potent enough for the Duke.

I glance at the ghostly light flickering within Vella's abdomen, then pull another stool up next to mine. "Come, sit. I've got a surprise for you."

She joins me. "But isn't—"

"He's still a little ways out. We've got time." Seventeen minutes to be exact, I think, but never say. "Close your eyes."

Vella clinks her brass eyelids shut.

"No peeking," I say, though my daughter has never peeked, not once in these six-and-a-half centuries. I pause in the interest of consistency, then reach under my workbench and flip a switch. Electricity arcs through the coils overhead, branches across the ceiling and leaps into the automaton I stashed behind a transformer some hours earlier. It sits up, stands, clomps over. "Okay. You can look."

She cocks her head. "It's...it's me?"

"Almost," I say.

"I don't understand."

I smile. Of the many moments we share time and time again, this one is my favorite, because she will never love me more than she will in this instant. "You've always wanted a little sister, right Vella?"

She jumps to her feet and her stool clatters to the floor behind her. "You mean..."

"I do. You can even pick her soul out yourself if you'd like. I doubt the Duke will miss just one."

She throws her arms around me, buries her face in my aluminum chest. "I actually get to go inside?" she says. "Oh, Father! Thank you! Thank you thank you thank you."

I squeeze her so tightly that her porcelain skin cracks beneath my fingers.

My heart revs, winds down; this will be the last time she hugs me.

I boot up my viewing screens and fiddle with the dials until Vella comes into focus, click-clacking across the wasteland with an empty jar cradled to her chest as if it's already precious.

Off in the desolation behind her, the city's clock towers loom like the teeth of some giant, half-buried gear. The Duke's dirigible bobs above them, smoking, a bloated fly that seems to swell with each breath I take.

Vella opens the outer hatch to the Soularium and gags at the stench that seeps out—as she always does—then slips inside.

I flip a toggle, and the stream jumps to the glass dome, where 144 humans dangle from ceiling-mounted chains in twelve orderly rows.

Solar panels jut wing-like from each of their backs, and hydration tubes snake down their throats. Simulators cover their eyes and ears and noses and mouths.

I tap the intercom. "Can you hear me?"

Vella's voice crackles back: "Father, what is this?"

"This is how souls are made, Vella."

"But they're—"

"Suffering? Of course they are. You can't forge a soul without pain. We've talked about this."

"But this is different, seeing them. This is so much worse than I thought it'd be."

"I know, sweetheart. I know. But best be quick. The Duke's almost here."

She stares down at her feet. "How do I know which soul to pick?"

"There's always some guesswork involved," I say, "but as far as people are concerned, the eyes are your best shot. Remember: the sharper the pain, the greater the sacrifice, the grander the soul."

"So..."

"You'll have to remove their visors to check."

"Ah."

"Think of your sister. We'll be a real family, Vella. That's what you want, right?"

She nods and sets the jar on the floor with trembling hands. "Alright. Okay." She steps up to a human and peels the simulator off his face. His bloodshot eyes find hers. He opens his mouth, but Vella slams the simulator back on before he has a chance to speak. "I can't do this. This is, this is—"

"You can. Try another one. Just one more."

Vella takes a shuddering breath and plucks another visor off a nearby human. This woman doesn't beg, doesn't scream. She doesn't even twitch. She just stares straight ahead, glassy-eyed, hollowed out.

As if on cue, Vella's hands curl into fists. She looks up into the camera, at me, with hardening eyes. "What do they see?"

"Whatever it is that they need to see."

"That's not enough," she says. "That's not even close to enough." She places the simulator to her own face.

This time, I remember to cut the audio a split-second before Vella screams. She drops to her knees, heaving, oil gushing out of her throat. I reconnect the audio.

The human looks on, unblinking, a scarecrow wrapped in sallow flesh.

Vella wipes the back of her hand across her oil-slicked lips. "Father, this isn't okay."

"No, but it's necessary. Please, Vella, take the soul—he's here."

Vella glances up through the glass ceiling, where the underbelly of the Duke's hulking dirigible is blotting out half the sky. "Does it ever stop?" she says.

"Does what stop?"

"After he harvests them. Does it stop? The pain."

"No," I say, the lie slipping smoothly off my tongue. "It never stops. But we need souls, Vella. Or there'd be no sisters, no children, nothing. We'd all be statues, shells."

Her eyes flick to the pyrolysis lever that's oh-so-conveniently mounted on the wall beside her.

I zoom in and watch her face. As always, I'm looking for aberrations, for some blessed malfunction in her code to base my hopes on. For a sign, however insignificant, that things aren't about to play out the way they always do. Because if Vella were defective, I might be able to justify keeping her. But once again, she's perfect.

"I know what you're thinking," I say, "but this is ten years' worth of work. Enough souls to populate a city. We're worth it, aren't we?"

"No," she says, and there is steel in her voice. "We aren't. Nothing should have to suffer like this." She wraps her delicate fingers around the lever.

"Please don't leave me," I say. Then, quieter: "not again."

Of the many moments we share, this is the one I despise most: the moment where —for the sixty-seventh time—Vella recognizes me for one infinitesimal part of the monster I really am.

"I still love you," she says, but she's always been a terrible liar. She squeezes her eyes shut and flips the switch.

Fire fills the dome. And just like that, it's over. What's left of the humans dusts the floor; their now-empty shackles swing freely from the ceiling; their souls scatter like cinders, reddening the glass where they flutter up against it.

But Vella still stands, glowing white-hot, her molten skin trickling down her frame and pooling around her feet.

And burning brighter than all of that— brighter than the flames, than the Duke's halogens, than even the stars themselves —is Vella's soul, a ball of liquid light that's illuminating her from the inside out.

"Father?" she says. "Why am I fireproof?"

"I'm sorry," she says again, as the Duke's ship touches down.

"You did the right thing," I say. "You always do the right thing."

"I don't understand."

"Every single time. I so wish you'd do the wrong thing, just once. Maybe then we'd have the sort of life we've always dreamed of. A real one."

"What do you mean, real?"

The cabin opens up and a ramp drops into the dirt. The Duke clatters towards us, just a head and torso mounted on eight spidery legs. Two of his automatons follow in his skittering wake.

"Is the girl ready for harvest?" the automatons say as one.

"She is," I say.

Vella presses a hand to her exposed abdomen. "You mean—it's my soul he's after? But—"

The automatons stomp towards her in lockstep.

"But I said I was sorry," Vella says. "Father, please! You still love me, don't you?"

"You served your purpose well," I say.

The automatons grab her by her arms and haul her away. I force myself to meet Vella's eyes. To watch her reevaluate the lie of a life I gave her. To watch her learn to hate me. The look on her face eviscerates what's left of my heart, just like it's supposed to.

A door seals shut behind her, and I know I'll never see that iteration of her again. The automatons will dispose of her body along with her soul; it, too, is much too weak for the Duke.

"Thank you, brother," the Duke says.

"I'm not doing this for you," I say, yet again, because it reminds me of what's at stake.

"I know," he says. "But I'm still sorry, for what it's worth."

I shrug and wipe my eyes, out of habit rather than necessity. I have no tears left to shed.

"I can't imagine reliving these same ten years," my brother says, "knowing this day will come." He presses a leg to my shoulder. "You're a hero back home, truly. Father would be proud."

I shake him off.

"Do you need a moment?" he says.

"I'm fine."

He nods. "Business then. I assume we're still on schedule?"

"We are." I pry my chest plate open and the Duke flinches away from the searing light that flares from me. My incandescence makes the dusky glow of his own failing soul seem utterly insubstantial; he has only eight-hundred years left at most.

"We must be getting close," he says, shielding his eyes with a thin pair of legs. "How many more loops before the donor soul's complete?"

"Twenty-two," I say, and the number leaves me leaden.

Twenty-two more Vellas; twenty-two more final hugs; twenty-two more I still love yous, all to delay my brother's death.

No—to prolong his rule. Because merciless as he might be, the Duke's hand is steady, and these last two millennia have been the most peaceful our clockwork city has ever known.

And because even after so many centuries, I can still picture Vella—the real, original Vella—crumpled on the sidewalk, her once-bright soul guttering around the fragments of her shattered chest. Vella, whose only crime was proximity to a riot she had no hand in.

I suck a breath through my aching throat. "How are things back home?"

"Tenuous," he says, "but manageable. Word's just gotten out that I won't be expiring as everyone expected—so the more ambitious factions are threatening revolution—but I've got it under control." He folds his legs underneath him and lowers himself to my level. "You'll come back with me once we're done here, won't you?"

"I should get the next loop going," I say.

He sighs, shakes his head. "As you wish. But tell me, brother: how do you do it?"

"Because when I do bring Vella back for good, I want there to be a world left for her to return to. Her future is worth the price."

"That's not what I meant. I founded nine new farms at the turn of this century, but none of them have yet to produce a soul that's lasted beyond two decades."

"Sounds like the farmers aren't taking to their offspring."

"Likely so. But how do you do it? How do you make yourself love them?"

"I've never had to try."

There is no laughter to be heard in my workshop now, no exaggerated sighs, no tapping of restless feet. Just a silence that feels not only smothering, but deserved.

I busy myself with the incinerator, starting with the belongings Vella left behind. Her decorative panels, her dolls, her colored irises. The clockwork dog I've always promised to bring to life but never have.

I'm about to burn her notebook when its weight gives me pause; it's heavier than ever before. I crack it open and flip through one familiar drawing after the next until I find the culprit: a piece of loose-leaf jammed between two pages. A new picture. The first ever aberration in the pattern since the Duke and I first set to harvesting my heartbreak almost seven-hundred years ago.

In her drawing, Vella and I are standing just outside the Soularium, and the Duke's dirigible floats a few feet off the ground. She and I are holding hands, and it is impossible to say whether the ship is landing or leaving.

The aberration is almost certainly nothing. It could just be a residual memory, a product of generational transference, some small corruption in the coding of her latest departed soul.

Regardless, I smooth the picture out and slip it into the drawer of my workbench. I've already decided that the dirigible she drew is taking off.

I snatch a copy of Vella's soul off the mantle and slot it into the automaton's abdomen. I dash back to my workbench and begin a diagnostic of her vital parameters, I test the articulation of her joints, calibrate her empathy levels until they're exactly where we need them.

I perform a surface-level debugging, but only that; I'm rushing things, and I know it. But I can't help myself. I flip a wall-mounted switch and electricity pours into Vella's doppelganger. It gasps and sputters to life.

"Hello, Vella," I say.

"Father?"

"Yes. Always."

See Kyle Kirrin's story "The Soul Farmer's Daughter" online at Metaphorosis.
If you liked it, leave a comment. Authors love that!

Remember to subscribe to our e-mail updates so you'll know when new stories are posted.

About the story

I really love time attack runs in video games (though I'm not particularly good at them), so I wanted to write a story where a character would be living—and reliving—a singular loop of events for an extended period of their life.

Originally, my plan was for the character to get better and better at the loop as time went on—sort of in the same vein as Edge of Tomorrow—but I ended up being more interested in what the character's life (and interior monologue) would look like if they weren't ever allowed to deviate from their past actions. Once that was all set, I figured I had to make the loop something awful to keep the narrative compelling, so I decided to have the main character repeatedly sacrifice his daughter's life. The character considers himself a monster for what he's done/what he'll have to do, though in the grand scheme of things he's doing everything he can to provide a future for his daughter.

To keep true to the origin of the story, I ended up having the vast majority of it take place within a seventeen-minute window at the very end of a loop.

Ultimately, my hope was that situating it that way would create the sense that the story is a very brief snapshot in time that gestures at a much larger whole.

A question for the author

Q: What was your favorite children's book?

A: *Ender's Game*, by Orson Scott Card. I've always been (and still am) a sucker for an underdog sports story, and Ender's Game pulled it off beautifully.

About the author

Kyle Kirrin lives at 9,000 feet above sea level in Creede, Colorado, where he tends to the needs of two Irish Wolfhounds and writes speculative fiction.

@KyleKirrin

The Bear Wife

Catherine George

The bear wife took the cub to mommy and me yoga. She didn't look much like a bear without her fur, but somehow the other mothers seemed to sense it; when she came in carrying the cub they shifted away, drifting on their yoga mats closer to the windows, to each other. She was left alone in the middle like a stone dropped into a lake, each woman a wave rippling outward. In tree pose she was a lightning-struck pine at the center of a clearing.

It must be something primal, she thought, lifting the cub up in a sun salutation. A smell, maybe, or a musk that hadn't gone away when the fur came off (worried now, she sniffed at her armpit as she twisted into warrior pose, but she smelled nothing but the plastic roses of her deodorant). Anyway, she didn't blame them for staying away. The bear was still in there, just below the skin; if any of them threatened the cub she'd tear the heart from their chest.

As the mothers eased into downward dog — a ring of A-frame cabins, each sheltering a baby — the weathered blonde yoga teacher approached her mat and placed a gentle hand on the bear wife's back, correcting her posture. "Like this," she said. "Keep your back flat." The hand pulled away, a bird taking flight, then settled again, on the hunch of her neck. "Focus on pulling the shoulder blades together behind you."

The bear wife didn't bother to tell her the hunch would never go away. No amount of focusing on her shoulder blades would remove the grizzly in her.

Once upon a time (about three years ago, but who was counting?), when the bear wife had been a real bear, she had done all the attendant bear-things: hibernating, rubbing her back on fir bark, scooping quicksilver trout from a chill alpine lake with one swipe of her paw. Now, her name was Sara and she bought organic and wore sunscreen to protect her weak skin from the sun.

She found herself thinking back on that once-upon time in the darkest hours of the night, when the cub was up and nursing, slow and dreamy. She too was slow and dreamy; she picked up her phone and pointed it to the place where the human mothers went: the babycenter forums, where BearMummy could ask about the color and quantity of the cub's poop, and receive seven answers in seven minutes. LOL that's totally normal, my bub went six times yesterday and it looked just like marmalade. But before she could navigate there, her mind slipped back into the old patterns, the bear-ways. The scent of her own cub's scat mixed with dry pine. The jammy squish of blackberries underpaw. The raw-throated awk awk of ravens, the sound of high summer.

Most surprising to her, at this three-years' remove (alright, so she was counting), was how short the list of things she'd done back then was, and how optional they'd been. Of course, bears had to eat, and hibernate, too, but she'd eaten when there was food and hibernated in whatever den felt right. Now she had a to-do list on her phone that said ping when she forgot to do something, which was often, because why would she want to remember to run the dishwasher, or get her legs waxed, or buy more soy milk? The phone did the remembering for her, ping ping ping. More diapers, it said. Vaccinations for Theo. And now, on doctor's orders: get out of the house.

"You can't just stay in bed all winter," the doctor had said when Sara told him they were hibernating. He said it as if it wasn't even an option. Truth be told, she'd begun to think it wasn't; they'd barely left the condo through the coldest breath of winter — barely left the bed, really — and she felt no better rested than she had after Theo was born. All she had to show for it was milk stains on the bedsheets.

"Go out, meet some mums, get some exercise," the doctor said impatiently. "It'll help you feel more like yourself again."

She remembered once seeing another mother with cubs across a valley bowl and turning right around to head back up above the tree line. No point in having too many cubs on the same territory, nosing after the same moths, hunting the same marmots. But apparently now other mothers were on the to-do list, so after yoga Sara watched the women nurse in the change room, comparing notes — "do you pump?" "how's her latch?" — while she huddled on a back bench and wished for a cool glade where she could lie down and feed the cub, instead of having to crouch awkwardly over him. She could never remember where to put her arms or his; somehow there was always an extra hand in the way. A wary look around showed all the others knotted together with their babies, too, like fallen logs tangled in the undergrowth on the forest floor.

The doctor was wrong, she thought. She'd never felt less like herself.

That night over sushi Aaron asked about the yoga. "So? You make any mum friends?"

He didn't say did you behave like a human today but that was what she heard; she was sure that was what he meant when he asked whether she'd been to the gym, or cooked the spaghetti al dente, or applied for a job at the pub around the corner. As if she were qualified to do that — as if she was qualified to do anything other than be a bear, really. Some things just seemed too human for her, no matter how she tried. Aaron didn't seem to understand that. He'd tried to teach her to drive, before she'd gotten pregnant. Two minutes in she'd seen a squirrel and driven right up the curb into a mailbox.

"Yeah, a few," she lied, and took a bite of dynamite roll. She loved sushi. She had mastered chopsticks as she'd once mastered the art of digging up lily bulbs, and learned to enjoy the heat of pickled ginger and wasabi tingling on her tongue. "I got some phone numbers."

"Oh?" Aaron gave her a skeptical glance. "So, what — you're going to take him on some playdates?" The cub in his bouncy chair batted at a toy. His concentration was ferocious.

"Yeah, maybe." Bears were not very good liars. Or maybe it was just her; she'd found it was better to say as little as possible, to avoid tripping over some human-thing she didn't know or understand. "Maybe we'll take them to the pool, go swimming."

Aaron said nothing, only took another avocado roll. She knew (that was why she'd said it, after all) that he was thinking of that other pool, the cold pool in the deep green shadow of firs. It was there he'd first seen her in human form: the bear maiden, bathing naked. It was there he'd found her fur.

In bed that night she pretended not to feel Aaron's hand running over the curve of her thigh, not to hear him whispering "Sara?" into the curve of her neck. His skin against hers felt raw, too close.

The bear wife and her husband went to couples' therapy.

"And does that make you afraid? About what it means for your relationship?" the therapist murmured, one eye on Theo, asleep in his carseat on the floor. They were talking about commitment. They were talking about how bears don't mate for life.

"I guess so, yeah," Aaron said. "It's like one day I'll wake up and she'll just be gone, back into the woods. I hate that it feels inevitable."

"Did you think about that when you met? That maybe she wasn't coming home with you forever?" the therapist said, gently. With her thick dark glasses and silvered hair, she looked like a raccoon, her little paws twisting together as she talked.

Aaron shrugged. "I mean, yeah, I suppose. I've heard the stories."

Sara knew the stories, too; she'd read hundreds of animal wife tales since she'd left her fur. The stories always blamed the husband for stealing fur or skin or feather. But she'd seen him running on that path before, often enough to know he might trip over her fur while she was bathing. The stories never said anything about how the wife might have wanted to come away for a while, either. Sara had wanted to come for — well, after all, why did anyone leave home? — adventure, love, maybe lust. He'd been handsome and lithe and when they lay together he'd nipped at her neck like a bear would. The stories never said anything about that, never said she might have wanted to see where things might go.

But of course things had gone just the way the stories said they would. There were always children, in the stories.

Aaron was still talking. "Once we said our vows I sort of thought things might be different."

"Hearing him say that, Sara — how does that make you feel?"

They had been over this territory before, so often she could almost see wary circling footprints in the dust of their conversation. "I'm still here," she muttered. "Isn't that enough?"

"Grizzlies abandon their cubs after two years," Aaron said to the therapist, casually, as if he was just giving her a science lesson. "Did you know that?"

"I did, actually," the therapist said. "Maybe you want to ask Sara if anything has changed for her, now that you two have a baby."

Sara could still remember the sound her cubs had made when she pushed them out to make their own lives: like rocks tearing, an earthquake of sorrow. When they'd tried to follow her, whimpering, she'd swatted them away, again and again, until finally they turned and slouched away over the hill. Every step they took away from her had been a thousand miles of heartbreak. It had been easier the second time, though, and the third. She glanced over at Theo, hiccupping in his sleep. She couldn't quite imagine letting his round cheeks out of the quick reach of her paws. But wasn't a cub a cub? Wouldn't she know how to leave him, when the time came?

"I shouldn't have to ask," Aaron said, angry, with an emphatic clang of his teacup on the plate. "I mean, don't you think —" Theo bolted awake with a growl, then began to wail.

"Well, I think that's time," the therapist said, with a sigh. "Should we pick up there next session?"

The cub woke again and again in the night, crying out for her. Sometimes Sara woke up dizzy, as if she were staggering out of the bearskin and back into her human form. She carried Theo from the bassinet into the bed, nestling against him so that his steady breath kept time against her chest, holding her in her skin.

In the morning Aaron groused about the size of the condo; there was only one bedroom for the three of them, which seemed right and usual to Sara, but left Aaron testy.

"I can hear him crying even with earplugs," he said, as he brushed his teeth before work. It surprised her that humans were so vain about their useless teeth, but she appreciated the mint flavor of the toothpaste. "I'll be falling asleep at my desk this afternoon."

"Let's get a bigger place, then," she said, shrugging.

"Can't afford it," he said. "Not on just one income."

Bears had no concept of personal property — each bear had a territory stamped out on the land, true, but the paths crossed and tangled and she remembered sitting with other bears to dig up little bean sprouts revealed by a glacier's slide — but more and more she'd felt hemmed in with the other bears, like seedlings choked for light on the forest floor. More bears in less space. Railway tracks on one side and a road on the other.

"Bears have a housing crisis too," she said to Aaron, and he laughed.

"At least they aren't paying two K a month for it."

She took the cub to visit the bones of the short-nosed bear at the natural history museum. The huge bear was frozen with one paw extended, spearhead claws slashing at empty air. Sara liked to come here to think; the skeleton felt like the closest thing she had to a relative in this city.

"Mama was never that big," she whispered to Theo, who had curled tight against her in the sling when faced with the bear's looming gaze. "And my teeth weren't that sharp, or my claws that long. You would have liked me." Well, she thought, that part probably wasn't true, but better he imagined her as cuddly. He squeezed her finger in one chubby fist, as if he understood.

The short-nosed bear had been extinct for twelve thousand years. She — the sign said the bones were from a female — had spent an eternity out of her fur.

"Did you get used to it, after a while?" Sara murmured. The bones didn't answer. They never did.

The stories all said she would go home again. That was the ending she'd expected when she'd come down from the mountains — for all she'd thought about it, at least. Really she'd just thought she'd play at human for a while. Had things changed? She pondered the therapist's question, wondering when exactly a change would have happened. When Theo had rushed out of her, squalling, naked and heavy? When the doctor had lifted him onto her deflated stomach, the weight of his body had hit like a rockslide. Now, when she cradled Theo's sleepy head against her chest, she felt the weight of time in her arms — four months old, now, and he wouldn't be full grown for years and years. So much longer than she'd spent with her other cubs, longer even than she'd been a bear. She hadn't expected that to matter.

As she turned to go to the exhibit on the invention of the steam engine she saw a dark-haired woman sitting on a bench near the children's fossil exploration station, one eye on a toddler digging in the sand. There was something familiar about her, or maybe about the look in her eyes — it reminded Sara of things she'd seen staring back from her own mirror. On impulse, she sat down on the other end of the bench. The other woman looked up and gave Sara an appraising look, then said, tentatively, "Bear?"

Sara nodded. "You?"

"Snow goose." Now she could see it, in the way the woman held her head tilted to one side, in the long reedy neck and thin lips. There was a sense of lightness that clung to her, as if a strong gust of wind could lift her, flapping, into the sky.

The other woman was called María and the toddler was Cora. María had gone home with a woman she'd met when her flock stopped over at the bird sanctuary on their way south to Mexico. Her wife was an airline pilot.

"She's away a lot," María said. "Goes all over the world."

"You miss it? Your life with the flock, I mean?" Sara asked.

"I must, because I dream about flying every night," María said. "And it makes me sad to think Cora will never have wings. And you? Do you miss it?"

"Yes," Sara said, automatically, then paused, thinking of the wildfires tearing through the forests, of the bears caught raiding the trash bins behind the new townhouse development, and relocated.

Or worse. Of the way the brutal roar of cars on the highway had silenced the scream of the lynx and replaced the tap tap tap of the woodpecker. "Sometimes," she said, slowly. "And sometimes not."

María nodded, as if she understood. The toddler came over and wordlessly offered Sara a fossilized fern. It looked a little like a feather, frozen in stone.

The bear wife took the cub to storytime at the library. The books at the library were insultingly off-base about bears. She liked honey fine but wouldn't be making a fool of herself over it, and the idea of wearing a duffel coat was laughable. Instead she showed Theo pictures of grizzlies in a travel magazine. He reached for them, then reared back, startled, as if expecting to feel fur between his fingers instead of slippery newsprint.

At the storytime she mouthed the words to row row row your boat while watching the other cubs; some could sit up and some could roll over and a few could pull themselves across the carpet, arm over arm, like beavers swimming in a pond. The other parents competed silently to see which baby could lie on their tummy longest without crying. When Sara put Theo down on his tummy he cried right away, surprised. She picked him up and pulled him against her, his ear on her heart. She knew how to teach many skills: how to raid a bird's nest, how to find the tastiest moths and white bark pine nuts, what a rifle shot sounded like from across the valley. How to pick a den by that ephemeral quality — the slant of light, maybe, or the curve of a fallen tree around the entrance — that made it match the taste of winter on the wind. Apparently she didn't know how to teach Theo to lie on his tummy.

"Mine didn't like tummy time either," whispered the closest mum, as if sharing a secret shame, like an acorn. Her baby was crawling now, an apex predator roaming among the other babies. Perhaps there was still hope for the cub.

After storytime she tagged along with the other mothers to a coffee shop, and drank an overpriced macchiato in an attempt to blend in, so she could offer Theo all the advantages that came with tummy time, with gymnastics lessons and sleep training. This time, after coffee, she got a few phone numbers.

María knew how to drive — "I drive stick, too," she said, proud — and offered to teach Sara. Nights, after the kids were in bed, they drove around and around the gravel lot at the bird sanctuary, dodging wood ducks, until Sara was confident she wouldn't be distracted by wildlife. When she swung María's little hatchback triumphantly out onto the road, the vibration of the pavement roared up through her feet, straight into her throat. Add it to the list of things she liked about being human, she thought. (An incomplete list: indoor plumbing, sleeping in, scalp massages, cappuccinos; the fact that she didn't need to worry about Aaron eating his own cub.)

Aaron's mother came to visit and clucked to herself while she watched Sara wrestle with Theo on the carpet, toppling him gently into a pillow, again and again, until he was fighting hiccups from laughing. She could remember wrestling like this with her other cubs, knocking them into the long grass with the back of her paw.

"He seems to like that, I suppose," Jillian said, sniffing. "But you know, dear, if you have questions about raising babies, you can come to me. It must be hard for you, fighting your instincts."

"Sara's a great mother, Mum," Aaron said, coming over to scoop Theo up and rolling his eyes. "She did raise six cubs, you know." Bears were smart, Sara thought, not to have mothers-in-law. Jillian had tried to insist they get married in a church, rather than the forest glade Sara had selected, and she'd spent the ceremony staring at the empty space reserved for the bride's family as if she were expecting bears to show up and trample the flower arrangements.

"Well of course, nobody's arguing about that," Jillian said, taking Theo and holding him carefully out at arm's length, as if she were trying to determine which parts of him came from the bear side of the family. "But it's different, isn't it?"

In truth, Sara didn't know what had happened to any of her cubs. Maybe they were all alive. Maybe they'd been hit by trains, though, or shot by poachers, or had starved in their dens after a lean summer. Maybe Jillian was right; maybe it was different.

Summer came, and with it the heat of the sun. Sara hid the cub in the stroller, covered him in sun hats, long sleeves, the slick squish of sunscreen. When she pushed him down the path to the playground the shade from each tree slapped her like a wet cloth. It bewildered her that humans were made so badly for living in the world outside. Sometimes at night when she lay beside Aaron, feeling the animal heat of him against her back, she marveled that he might die if she locked him outside naked overnight.

The same thought overtook her when she looked down in the purple twilight at Theo sleeping restlessly in his crib, legs twitching up and slumping down: this crib, this onesie, these walls and windows, all bulwarks built up against the death that lurked outside, waiting. She could never take him to nestle down at the base of a burnt-out stump all night. Instead she watched him nap on the video monitor, counting his breaths in infrared.

She took the cub to storytime, again and again. One day Theo was the baby that roamed the library, crawling. He was fast on all fours; he got that from her. At the playground Sara discussed sleep training and nap schedules with the other parents. One day Theo was the baby that slept through the night. When the mums chatted about their lives before children she found herself saying "I'm a — well, I was a bear, once." There was an owl dad in their playgroup, and a seal wife at swimming lessons. That seemed like an unfair advantage, she thought as she tried and failed to get Theo to put his face underwater.

"I think you're better at parallel parking than I am," Aaron said, when she drove them to the farmer's market to get peaches and arugula and croissants.

"Oh, I definitely am," she said. "You'd better let me teach Theo to drive, when he's old enough."

The headlines were full of bears. A bear had been spotted on the beach at the lake, rooting through coolers, demolishing picnic hampers. The park ranger set out a trap but, the paper reported, "the crafty beast managed to avoid capture." Sara chuckled at this, but the other stories were not so funny: a hiking trail was closed after a dog was mauled; a hunter shot a large grizzly that was a mainstay of photography tours. So-called "problem bears" were everywhere. But really, she thought, the stories were full of problem humans, like the terrible children who threw bread and apples to a bear who came into their back yard, so that the bear returned again and again, like a lapdog ("the fate of the bear is unknown, as conservation officers are assessing whether it can be safely relocated").

At breakfast, she saw Aaron hastily drop the paper, slide the news under last night's pizza box. He avoided her eye, busied himself with offering the cub half a blueberry.

"What was that?"

"What?" he said, all puzzlement. Theo squealed and shook his high chair reaching for the berry. "What was what?"

After Aaron went to work, she dug out the paper and found the story: a mother grizzly on the coast had mauled a man who lumbered too close to her cubs, trying to take a photograph. She had to be shot. For a long time after reading Sara sat holding Theo close, face buried in the moss-soft fuzz on his head. He whimpered and squirmed, trying to slip loose to crawl after a stray toy on the floor. She held him tighter, until he calmed and fell asleep against her, sweat pooling in the space between their hearts.

The story did not say what happened to the cubs.

Sara found herself thinking about the animal-wife stories a lot, mostly about the endings. She thought about them when she was reading to Theo at night, when she was feeding him cubes of sweet potato, when she was driving him over to a friend's house for a playdate. She told herself that all the stories agreed that it would be years before she went back, years and years. Her sense of human time was terrible — Aaron was always complaining about how she was late for appointments, for their dates — but she could feel the turning of the seasons. There would be time still to show Theo how to find the ripest huckleberries on the bush, and time to see him learn to talk, and hear him call her mama.

On the phone with María, Sara asked if she knew the stories.

"Of course," María said. "Doesn't everybody?"

"Have you — have you ever looked for your feather cloak?" Sara hadn't looked since Theo's birth; she'd looked before, a few times, even though she knew that wasn't how things worked, that she needed a child to find it for her. Of course, nothing had ever turned up, not in the backs of the cupboards or behind the dryer or in the air vents, and she'd lacked the tools to bust up the drywall.

"No. Not yet."

"Will you, though? One day?"

There was a long pause and Sara could hear Cora, in her bright birdsong voice, asking for a cup of milk. Then María came back on the line. "I don't know. Sometimes I hope she's flown it to the other side of the world."

Sometimes, on the weekends when she and Aaron took the cub out for a walk, she caught herself rubbing one hand over the bark of the maple trees in the boulevard, or staring too long at the distant blue smear of the mountains. On those days, Aaron tried hard to distract her, cooking her salmon on the barbecue and bringing home shiny baubles.

"I'm not a crow, you know," she complained to the therapist, after the third pair of silver earrings.

The therapist laughed. "Why don't you guys try something new? Try going outside, getting back to your roots. Go camping, or something."

The bear wife and her husband took the cub camping. At the site Aaron set about pitching the big orange tent, over-enthusiastically pounding in the pegs in and exclaiming over the view of the lake that lay shimmering mirror-grey beyond the gaps in the alders.

"This is the perfect campsite," he said, bang bang bang. "The breeze off the lake will keep the bugs off, and he can practically crawl down to the beach." Theo was crawling around the picnic table, batting at imaginary animals and squawking in triumph. "See," Aaron grunted, now huffing up and down on the pump for the air mattress, "I told you he'd like camping."

Sara went to the woodpile to get logs, so that they could cook beans over a crackling fire and roast potatoes in the coals, because according to Aaron that was the thing to do while camping. When she stood up with an armful of cedar they were there, by the garbage bins, pawing at the bear-proof lids: a mother with two cubs, yearlings. Just feet away. In the heavy shadow under the firs, their eyes threw back the sun like highbeams. For a second she was frozen, staring. Was staring a no-no for bear safety, Sara wondered, or was it just not polite? When she made a little choked growl at the absurdity of her own thoughts, they all turned to look at her. The mother bear whuffed and stood up, towering over the bins. Sara held her gaze, manners be damned, to look for something she couldn't name — maybe just her own bear-self reflected in the dark mirror of those eyes. But there was nothing there, nothing but hunger.

"Go on, scram," she said, softly, after a moment. "Get out of here before they catch you digging in there and relocate you." The mother snorted and dropped to the ground, butting the cubs with her head, prodding them north.

When she came back to the campsite she was shaking. Aaron put down the pump and left the mattress hissing like a garter snake. "Are you alright? Maybe this camping thing was a bad idea."

"No, I'm fine," she said. "I'm — I'll be fine." She turned and picked up the nearest thing, blindly. It turned out to be the axe. "I'll just chop the wood, I think."

Long after she had chopped, after they'd all splashed in the snowmelt cold of the lake, after they'd finished eating those beans and potatoes, Sara lay awake listening to the sounds of the lake and the forest beyond. Once, the wind in the firs had been her lullaby. Now her ears felt empty, waiting for the whoop-whoop of the ambulance siren, the screech of tires on pavement, the humming thrum of the city at night. She heard the blatting honk of a lone goose in the wind above, and took some solace in the fact that there was a space for honking in both her worlds.

When Aaron leaned over and nuzzled her neck and murmured "Are you awake?", Sara rolled towards him and unzipped her sleeping bag. His legs tangled against hers and the sound of their breathing grew to fill the silence.

The cub found the fur in the lining under the couch. He was digging around for a ball, yelling ba ba ba, when he caught one hand in the lining and pulled it loose. The smell smacked Sara from fifteen feet away, unmistakable, like a hard north wind: a faint tinge of wildfire layered on marsh grasses, sedge, and cow parsnip. Blood, and the metallic tang of snow. She stood there for a heartbeat, staring at the dense brown fur hanging from Theo's hand, and felt nothing but static. Then, with a breath, she was furious. Of all the places to hide it, he'd chosen this? Where she would sit on it every day, where she would shove around with the vacuum cleaner? It should've been in a storage locker somewhere, she thought, as she dragged the four-inch claws out of Theo's greedy grasp. That or in the ceiling panels of his office downtown, or — well, anywhere but here.

She was supposed to have years before the end of the story. It was supposed to take her forever to find it.

The bear wife put on the fur. It smelled like the inside of the couch, dust and leather. Pulling it on felt like twisting into an old sweatshirt that had shrunk in the dryer, tight in all the wrong places; she wiggled a bit, tugging at the shoulders, and then —

Now she crouched in this too-small place. Not cozy like a den. Clinging, like ivy strangling a tree. The sky too close. A smell: bee-stuff. She pawed at the smell until the strange tree ripped under her claws. This little space like a trap. The bee-stuff was in a hive — a jar, a voice whispered. It fell, broke. She licked it up. You'll have to clean this up later, you know. More smells. She clawed again; the old-food poured out. Food left too long in the sun. Should've been buried. Oh, god, not the compost — She ate it anyway. Now time to scent. Time to scratch.

A sound. A cry. He's waking up, he's hungry, he needs you — A small, mewling thing lay there. Like moth larvae, wiggling and screaming. She reached for it, claws out. No! This is your cub, you can't —

A moment suspended between bear and woman:

The smell of sedge grass, scat, deep-summer salmonberries.

Theo's sweet milk breath, and the warm soft scent of his head in her arms, like flat champagne.

The taste of thistles in late spring. Sun pooling in her fur.

Theo's eyes wide with joy at his first taste of blackberries. Aaron's arm curling warm around her shoulders.

Then Theo screamed again, the cry of a cub abandoned by his mother —

She stopped. Turned the claws on herself, and tore.

Afterwards Sara sat topless in the dark, the cub nursing greedily at her breast, the torn fur at her feet. The smell of the compost, fertile and rotten, echoed out of the kitchen. The broken glass she could sweep up, but she thought the cupboards were probably a lost cause. The fur — well, she would find a space for it, somewhere. Clawing it off had felt like giving birth to Theo all over again: a great glorious moment of splitting in two, of bringing something new into the world. A new ending to her story, she thought. A million new endings, even, and any of them could be hers.

She gathered the fur into her arms, folded it carefully, and put it away in the closet with the spare quilts.

*See Catherine George's story "The Bear Wife"
online at Metaphorosis.
If you liked it, leave a comment. Authors love
that!
Remember to subscribe to our e-mail updates so
you'll know when new stories are posted.*

About the story

The first line of this story popped into my head while I, like the bear wife herself, was up in the middle of the night nursing a two-month-old baby. Around that time, I'd been researching local baby and mum yoga classes and reading animal wife and selkie stories, so apparently my sleep-deprived brain mashed the two together. I wrote the line down on my phone in the dark and in the morning found myself thinking about what modern parenting would look like to someone who had grown up in the animal world, as well as how the animal wife story might change if it happened in a contemporary setting.

A question for the author

Q: What would your characters say about you?

A: I like to think that Sara, the bear wife, would want to be part of my parent friend group, but I suspect she would tease me for my city-bred ways and middling outdoor survival skills. (Like Aaron, her husband, I enjoy trail running, but unlike him I've never seen a grizzly while running – just black bears.) She would probably also note that I'm really, really bad at yoga, whether with a baby or without.

About the author

Catherine is a lawyer living in Vancouver, BC with her partner and two young children. She began writing again after more than a decade off during the maternity leave for her second child, and now writes all types of speculative short fiction.

cgfiction.com, @catinlaw

Mean Streak

L'Erin Ogle

The air is dry and brisk, the leaves curled at the edges and hanging limp in shades of red, gold, and brown, dying as the sun edges farther away every day. It's the kind of day made for hanging witches. That's what Jasper says, at least. His father's the law around here. He and his men found an entire coven of them, hunkered down in a house hidden in the forest, acting like they were normal people. Tonight, they will hang all of them. You don't ever wait to hang a witch. History has all kinds of lessons about that.

Daddy hurries us down the road, away from town and the square, away from the gallows. The bottom of the sun touches down on the horizon, burning the rest of the day out. I can hear all of them, chanting together. It's always the same kind of things—burn the witch, hang the witch, kill them all. Over and over, until the chant turns into a melody that crawls inside and whispers to a secret place inside of you. Makes you want to be part of it.

We're past where the road turns from gravelly rock into dry dirt, where whirlwinds rise up and circle around the horses' hooves with each step, when Daddy's horse jigs right and stops dead, pawing at the ground. Daddy pats her neck, tells her to go easy. She's got her ears pricked up, listening. Then I hear it. A sound that makes every hair go sharp in its follicle, stand wire straight off the skin. It's soft and rhythmic, a chuff chuff chuffing full of strangled agony. Then two skeletal arms, streaked with dried rusty blood, reach over the edge of the road. The palms plant against the dirt, the bloody fingers dig grooves, the arms strain to form right angles at the elbows. I follow the arms to the shoulders appearing, to the matted hair, thick with great viscous clots that shine and wink at something dark inside me.

The hair hangs over its face, the arms tremble as it lunges forward, and the pale naked flesh of it flops against the road. A hole large enough to accommodate my fist gapes on its side, wide lipped and ruby red, and through the open mouth of it peers a dirty white sickle-curved rib.

It crests the ditch, dragging rusty, bloodstained legs behind it. The smell of copper hangs heavy in the air around it, assaults the back of my nose with the stench of it. Dirt sticks to blood that is still wet, blood that falls in drops from the wound in its side. I think it's a woman but it's hard to tell, the way the chest is pressed to the road, the amount of filth it wears. It is hardly even recognizable as a human, really.

Daddy dismounts, hands the reins to Tillie. Tillie is sixteen and I am fourteen, the years between us vast as oceans. Different fathers make us different seasons. Tillie chews the inside of her cheek, her body wired tense, her face turned small and pinched. She's like Mamma, that way. Everything rings through her louder.

"Hey," Daddy says. He takes slow, even steps up to it.

I ride up next to Tillie to get a better look.

Daddy gets right up next to it and crouches down. He's tall and skinny; folded up he looks like a bundle of sticks. He reaches out, and puts his hand on its shoulder, away from that awful thing on the side that glitters open, a secret door into the body. The thing screeches—it humps up its body like a worm, curling away and still trying to contract, wiggle away to another place.

"Easy," Daddy says, same tone he just used to soothe his horse. "Easy, there." He puts his hand on the shoulder of the thing, halts its nonexistent forward progress. From under the mass of knotted hair, the thing turns and makes a sound I have never heard, one of anguish and fear and even a note of pleading all wound up in there.

I realize I have held my breath in my chest, as the neck of it rotates and the hair falls away from the face, and it burns in my chest as the bluest sky eye comes out from under. A sharp blade nose, pale lips, and the other eye, silver iris, black pupil.

"Witch!" I cry out.

"Hush," Daddy snaps without looking back, stinging me whip sharp.

"Easy," Daddy says, to the thing. The witch thing. "We're not going to hurt you." It trembles and moans. I'm fairly certain it's a woman, the curve of a breast just visible if you look close enough.

She doesn't have any clothes, but everything private's covered with blood and dirt. Daddy strokes her shoulder gentle but still she flinches, her eyes running mad in their sockets, her fingers scrabbling for holds in the road. They're all bloody at the end, bent in funny ways, missing some fingernails.

"Someone'll be coming," Tillie says, looking around. "Maybe she got away from the hanging."

"She's not from the hanging," Daddy says. "Not like this."

"Still, someone's gotta be looking for her," Tillie says.

"I know," Daddy says. He gets up. Tillie's already digging in her saddlebag. They talk without talking, like he's her real dad instead of mine.

Tillie pulls out a ratty old blanket out of her bag and hands it to Daddy. He eases it around the witch thing, real nice.

She doesn't respond now, her fingers move restlessly through the dirt, her eyes stare off at something else. She whines when he scoops her up, but it doesn't last long either. When he carries her to his horse, her arms and legs hang scarecrow limp.

He hoists her up, his arms shaking from the effort, drapes her across the saddle, swings up behind the saddle, which startles his horse. He has to lean over it to grab the reins. He looks right at Tillie.

"Stay on the main road," he says. "Stay with your sister. Go straight home, hear?"

Tillie nods. He looks past her to me. "Listen to your sister, Winnie."

With that, he turns his horse right and disappears into the trees, taking the back-way home.

"Come on," Tillie says, the second he's out of sight. She guides her horse around the mess it made, the pool of blood and dirt shaped like a three quarters moon. I can smell it, damp and invasive and rich. I fall behind her, aiming to ride right over it, but Bonnie dances around it, the horse version of tiptoeing.

"This is wrong," I say, nudging Bonnie to go faster, til I can look Tillie right in the eye, but Tillie stares straight ahead, the skin on her face drawn taut by tension. "Helping a witch is the same as being one."

"That don't make it right." Tillie says.

"If someone finds out," I persist, "we'll hang too."

"Dad would," she corrects me. "We're too little and we ain't got nothing to do with it."

She calls him Dad even though he isn't. Her dad passed when she wasn't even born yet, caught the wasting sickness. I guess Daddy's the only daddy she's ever had, but it still rubs me the wrong way, sandpaper on raw nerve endings.

"Well." I can't think of anything else to say. Tillie and I, we just aren't the same kind of people.

"You haven't ever seen a hanging," she says, real soft.

"And you have?"

"Once I was at Grace's, didn't know they were gonna have one. They caught her trying to steal something, I guess, hung her up right aways, in the square. Grace and I didn't even want to watch, but we couldn't get people to let us through, to get out."

"You seen it? Did she try to get away?"

Tillie shook her head. "She knew it was over. She just stood there. Let it happen. I closed my eyes, and I heard everything go really still and silent, and then I heard the wood moving, heard the wind shift. There was this awful plop, plop, plop. I opened my eyes and she was just dangling there, like a doll. Her eyes were open but they had clouds over them."

"What was the plops?"

"She shat herself," Tillie says. "It was awful. It was the very worst thing that could ever happen."

"Did her tongue stick out?" I want to know. Jasper and the others, they say the tongue comes sticking out and birds peck it out, they say the face turns mottled purple, they say crows roost in the tree and watch.

"Shut up," Tillie says, and doesn't say another word.

Daddy's horse is tethered to the post in the yard. The back way is through the woods, where the ground shifts beneath you. It's faster, but Daddy says it's only safe for people who have ridden as many years as him. Tillie tells me to unsaddle and put up the horses, just like I knew she would. Dad tells Tillie what to do, she tells me what to do, and I just get the short end of the stick, every time. By the time I'm done, all the light's been sucked out of the sky. The fire's lit, beckoning as soon as I open the door. Aunt Caro is in her wheeled chair, dunking ripped up sheets into a boiling pot. Her biceps flex with muscle, the same muscle that hoists her in and out of her chair every day. She was born with thin legs that refused to carry her and now they are little more than sticks attached to her body.

Tillie's room door is open and I can see Daddy and Tillie beside a pallet, where it lies.

"What are they doing?" I ask Caro.

"Trying to clean up, put on some bandages," Caro says. She reaches down and gets a bowl, uses wooden tongs to spoon out the linens and drop them in. She tells me to take the bowl to Daddy. I walk in and it smells of fermented fruit and sweat, oily and slick in my mouth.

Tillie's doing the cleaning. Daddy's using his fingers to feel around the wet side wound. I push the bowl next to him.

"What are you doing?" I whisper. I don't want to talk too loud, because the whole room feels unsteady, blurred at the edges, like maybe one wrong word will cause the witch to rise up, cast spells.

"Making sure nothing's in there," he whispers back. "Cleaning it out best I can. Don't want to close it with anything in it."

"How are you gonna close it?"

"Sew it up." He takes a wet, steaming cloth, and pushes it inside the wound. Squeezes it and the water runs out, dark with blood and dirty water. He does it a few times until it's mostly clear. Then he dips his hands in the water and cleans them. He's got big hands with long slender fingers. Everything about Daddy is long and thin. He takes the edges of skin with thumbs and first fingers, uses the others to smooth the rumpled-up flesh. That little curved rib shines at me, looking silk smooth. Then he pinches the skin together with one hand.

"Hand me that," he says, about the needle and thread next to me. I do. He already pushed the thread through the eye of the needle, and he pricks it through the skin, one side to the other, drawing it tight, sealing it up.

I watch him for a while. He does it well, like everything else. "Where'd you learn that?" I ask.

"My grandma was a healer," he says.

"Like a doctor?"

He laughs quietly. "There weren't any doctors in her time. So, yes, in a way."

The thing whimpers a little while he works. But after a while, her eyelids ease closed. She's silent the rest of the time. They cover her with blankets and maneuver her pallet beside the fire.

Daddy sends me and Tillie to bed, and I lie in bed thinking about hangings and bones and mouths carved into skin while Daddy's and Aunt Caro's mutterings dance just outside the edge of my hearing.

She sleeps for near three days straight. Aunt Caro and Daddy keep us away from her, move Tillie into my room. Around the corners of doors, I can see them spooning liquids and broth into her mouth, her kitten-weak swallowing. Once, I see her neck, dark purple mixed with blue black, bruises in the shapes of hands and fingers, once I see the ladder tracks of Daddy's stitches pulled tight across swollen red skin, leaking pus, once I see Daddy push her hair off her face and my heart turns to stone in my chest, dense and solid and impenetrable.

The fourth day, she is sitting at the table, wearing one of Tillie's dresses. It is short, falling halfway down her thigh instead of the knee. There are fading bruises scattered along the curves of her calves, even on her long, narrow feet. Her arms are sticks decorated with the same berries of color, shaped like fingers and wrapping all the way around the biceps and forearms. They must have cut her hair off, and what's left dusts the top of her shoulders, dark and glossy. Her eyes are clear and cold, the silver and blue irises moving liquid under the sunlight pouring through the window. Aunt Caro and Tillie both sit at the table, Daddy leans against the wall. The air is still and quiet, but something quivers underneath it, something I can't quite grasp.

"Of course, you're free to go," Daddy says. "But there are men everywhere looking for your kind. You're welcome to stay here a while longer, out of sight. Regain your strength."

The witch, young, not one of the wrinkled crones that I imagine dangling from nooses, cocks her head, perched on her thin stalk of a neck. "And what would be the cost of that?"

Her voice is raspy. The necklace of purple remains vivid, unlike the other marks that fade. When she speaks, she passes her hand up to press against her throat.

Daddy doesn't answer but he shakes his head just once. His eyes are sad eyes, always, since Mama died, but today the depth of it grates to look at, so I glare at her. Then he says, with so much kindness in his voice it sets my jaw to aching, "There isn't a price. We aren't the kind of people who believe in harming others."

Maybe *they* don't, I think to myself. Something glitters in me that is mean and sharp and real as the hair on my head, real as the witch in our house.

"You're a man," she says. "What do you require?"

"Nothing," he says, shakes his head. "I'm not that kind of man."

There is an understanding reached between them, something that passes between them like the notes others pass in class, the ones I don't ever get.

"You'll have to stay out of sight," Daddy says. "We don't get much company, but, still."

"Of course," she says.

"The first snow," he says. "The men will be busy shoring up the barns, covering the fields. It will be a good time to leave. It should come soon, maybe a month."

She nods again. When she stands up, she presses her hand to her side. And somehow, between the four of them, it's all settled.

My jaw throbs, my teeth clenched together tight.

"What's your name?" Tillie asks.

Caro made me and Tillie go pluck green beans this morning. I hate it. They're all bunched together low to the ground and hard to pull off. Dirt sneaks up under my nails and makes them gritty for days no matter how much I wash them. When we sit down to break off the stems, Milla comes right over and lowers herself beside Tillie, her breath hissing out between her teeth. We work in silence until Tillie decides she wants to have a get-to-know-the-witch session.

"Milla," she says. Milla only speaks when she's asked a question. "Where are you from?"

"Right here."

"Did you have a mom and dad?"

Tillie's asking questions like a witch really has a beginning. I haven't ever heard of them having beginnings, only endings.

"A mother," she says.

"Where is she?"

Milla snaps a bean right in half. She puts it down. Her hands are smooth and most of her fingernails are already growing back. They tremble, just a little bit.

"Dead," she says. "Hung a long time ago."

"Our momma died too," Tillie says.

My stomach tightens into a knot, strings pulled tight all across my body.

"She was real pretty," Tillie says. "She got the wasting sickness when Winnie was just a baby. She was always laughing."

Her face turns blurry. I rub my eyes with my fists. I don't have memories like Tillie. I don't have any images of my mother pasted in my head I can flip through. When I think about it, I feel cold as wet river stones inside, and my teeth set against each other.

"I think that's enough beans for now," Aunt Caro says. When I look at her, deep lines have been drawn in her forehead, ones that don't disappear later.

I hear the softest voice that night, lying in bed. It's her, talking to herself, but I can't make out what she's saying. There's a sound accompanying it, something that could be mistaken for crying, if I didn't know that witches don't cry.

She has been here for seven days and seven nights the night I get up for a drink. I come around the corner, see Daddy leaned back in his chair, his face falling off the planes of his bones. He looks old, like maybe time has passed I didn't know about it. If I were a different kind of girl,

I'd go crawl in his lap and put my arms around him, but I can't, because I have a mean streak inside me. It's sharp and crackling like a bullwhip.

But then there are soft footsteps, and Daddy's eyes snap open. He sits up, his face coming all together again. Then Milla the witch moves towards him. She's wearing one of Tillie's shirts, that hardly covers her private bits.

"What are you doing?" Daddy asks her. He swallows and I can hear it loud, even over my heart thumping double in my chest.

"I owe a debt to you," she says. "I know you say you don't require it, but I don't want it hanging over my head." The shirt drops down her back, off her arms, lands puddled on the floor. She is still thin, but curvy in parts, skin like polished ivory. Something fat and ugly lodges in my throat.

Daddy's skin has gone white, his hands grip the arms of the chair so tight the veins on the back of his hand bulge out. He's shaking his head. "No," he says.

"I owe you," she says. "I can make you —"

"No," Daddy says. He stands up fast, snatching a blanket off the back of the chair. "Go back to bed, Milla." He puts the blanket around her front first, and I can see his hands shaking when he wraps it around the back.

He keeps his eyes to the side, not looking at her.

"Is it because of them, what they done?" she asks. Her voice isn't quite as strangled as it used to be, just husky.

"Nothing to do with that," he says. He turns away, and I can hear both their hearts beating and colliding in the air around them. "Please go, Milla." Like his hands, his voice shakes.

I do not get a drink. I do not think it would pass the lump in my throat.

I grind my teeth to drown out the drums of beating hearts pulsing in my eardrums.

It does not snow for two weeks. Tillie keeps asking Milla questions, Milla answers. She says she can't do any magic. That she wasn't ever taught. That she just wants to live in peace.

Witches lie. Ask anybody.

"She's pretty, isn't she?" Tillie asks me.

Milla's standing at the window. She's still wearing Tillie's clothes. They might be the same size around, but Milla's tall and it seems like her legs and back are always exposed. She is pale and her bones are sharp under her skin and sometimes I catch Daddy watching her move fluidly across our house, looking all twisted up.

It isn't the first time I've seen Daddy look at a woman like that. There have been others. One, Amy, even came to dinner a few times. She had a laugh that scraped across the nerve endings in my ears. She lasted longer than the others, but she left too. I used to throw fits. I'd scream and kick and bang my head against the floor. I imagined me scraping right back across her eardrums and her head pounding like mine.

"I can't do this," she told Daddy after one.

"Aren't you lonely?" I overheard Caro ask him one night.

I was glad I was eavesdropping and couldn't see his face. Hearing all the pieces of his voice was bad enough. "I miss my wife," he said. "I don't think anything can make that kind of lonely go away."

There was no one else until Milla. I'm older, so I know I won't get away with fits like I used to. I glare at her; don't eat anything she's touched. Today, I tripped her, Daddy moving lightning quick to catch her, and she made an odd strangled sound and recoiled from him. She fled with her hand against her side and didn't come out the rest of the night. Tillie gave me a mean look, but her meanness doesn't have nothing on me. she knows it, too.

I creep out after I hear Caro's chair squeak to her bedroom, after Tillie's breathing is deep and regular and she doesn't hold her breath when my sheets rustle. I peer around the hall corner, where I see Milla, no top on. She clutches a shirt to her chest. I see Daddy on his knees. For a moment, I think the worst, but then I see the scissors in his hand, sharp and silver. He's severing the threads he put in, is all, and it gets easier to breathe.

She doesn't move, even when it must hurt, except to wrinkle her forehead. When he removes the last one, he touches her on the pink seam he created. "Hurt?"

She shakes her head. "I'm sorry," she says.

I can feel how they're looking at each other then. How thick it is between them, how there's another secret circle I won't ever belong to.

"About what?" he says.

"Earlier. I was just startled, you know," she says. Her voice drops lower in register. Daddy hitches a breath in. Out. "It's going to be time for me to go soon, isn't it?"

I think Daddy says yes but he's so close to a whisper I can't rightly make it out.

"I was thinking." She stops. Moisture, the pale imitation of a tear, glistens in her blue eye. "I was thinking about the things they did to me. I was thinking someone might do it to me again, probably. And I was thinking maybe if I had something nice to remember, maybe I could forget some of it, block it out."

Daddy's breath comes out all at once. He stands up, knitting his hands together.

"Not payment," she says. "Not at all."

"Oh," Daddy says, hoarse.

"Please," she says and then she puts her mouth, her enormous blood red mouth, on his. I can hear their hearts banging away again. Together, crashing and booming in thunderous blasts. I can't quite take it, but I can't look away. She drops the shirt, and Daddy's arms go around her. She's tugging at his, and they separate to let it over his head, and her breasts are small and round and the nipples tip them pink. Daddy drops his mouth to one, and Milla groans and then there's something inside me burning and hollering, and I take my hand into my mouth and clamp down so hard I taste my own blood, just to keep from screaming. I feel my stomach knotting up and squeezing and I know my dinner's fixing to reveal itself, and I do turn away, I do, I do.

Rage builds a house inside me.

Snow comes and Milla doesn't leave. She smiles now, a wicked wanton scythe, looking at my Daddy, braiding Tillie's hair. Helping Aunt Caro. I can hear them at night. I know what they're doing, but it isn't the sex stuff that bothers me. It's the way he looks at her that sets my bones afire.

Winter is here, white spread over dead trees and dead fields.

We go outside and the cold sets my nose to numb, matches my insides. I don't feel anything at all when I walk up to Jasper.

"Jasper," I say. "Gotta talk to you."

Jasper tosses his hair, just like a girl. "What do you want?" His breath comes out cool and shimmering, pretty like the rest of him.

"Alone," I say.

All the times Milla makes me mad stack up on each other. The mean streak trembles and it wants her to go away. I want that too, but I feel fingers, ghost cold, trying to seize my words before they come out. They feel like I imagine a mother's touch would, but I shake them off. If the gods wanted me to have a mother, they would have let me keep mine.

Jasper rolls his eyes. "All right, horseface," he says. He walks around the building with me. "What?"

He crosses his arms in front of him. "Interested in showing your daddy a witch?"

He thinks it over. He doesn't have much use for me, but he's the youngest of three boys. He sure does want his daddy's attention. I know all about that.

"Where?" he asks.

"Gotta promise me one thing," I say. I make tears appear in my eyes. I brush at them with dirty snowflakes on my fingertips, help the process along. I start leaking good. "My daddy doesn't get hurt. See, there's a witch possessed my daddy. Laid a spell right on him, and Aunt Caro, too. You gotta promise you won't hurt them."

"Yeah, all right," Jasper says. I can see the flush of excitement crawl up his cheeks. "I guess I can take care of your witch problem for you."

"You promised, Jasper. No harm to my Daddy."

"Yeah, sure," he says, but he's forgotten me, moving around the corner.

Inside, I taste something rich and sweet spreading through me.

Milla and Daddy are walking past each other, getting the table ready for dinner, brushing their finger together, eyes like moons. I'm sick and miserable, wanting the knock at the door to come. I'm on the outside, looking in, as always.

But it's Tillie spilling through the door first, pale and high spots of color in her cheeks. She looks right at me. "You told!" she shouts and then slams into me. We fall to the ground and she's swinging her fists one two one two, raining them against my head.

Then Daddy's got Tillie around the waist, pulling her back. "What the hell's going on, Tillie?" he shouts.

"She told about Milla!" Tillie screams, and she's crying real tears. Not like mine or Milla's.

Daddy looks at me, and I put my fist in my mouth and bite down hard.

"Oh, Winnie," Caro says. She twists the blanket in her lap between her knotted hands.

Daddy looks at me. His face cracks like glass. Then he looks away, dismisses me like I'm not even there.

"You have to go," he says to Milla. "Right now."

Milla has manufactured tears. They slide down her cheeks and drip onto shoulders. She holds out her thin, angular arms to him and then he crosses the room and wraps her up in them. I know she's going but still feel my hate inside me, expanding and spreading and I saw my teeth against each other.

"I'm sorry," he says, pressing his lips against her forehead. "I'm sorry, I'm sorry, I'm sorry."

"Ssshh," she says. "It's alright. We knew it would happen. We'll meet again." She draws his mouth down to hers. He's crying too, something he only does when the memory of Momma chews at him too hard. She lets him go, and turns to Caro and squeezes her hands tight. "Take care, Caro," she says.

"Be safe," Caro says. She's crying too. Everyone is but me.

Tillie runs and throws her arms around her. Milla hugs her back and whispers to her. Tillie shakes her head back and forth. Milla kisses the top of her head. She starts toward me and I feel my insides contract. She stops but doesn't touch me. She looks into my eyes with her mismatched set. "Take care, Winnie," she says. "I don't blame you."

It makes me feel even more knotted up and angry inside. I open my mouth but nothing comes out.

And then Daddy is beside her, telling her to take his horse, telling her she has to hurry. They disappear through the door together. I want to follow, to see what happens next, to see it through to the end, but Tillie comes right up to me, her fists balled up at her sides.

"What the hell is wrong with you?" she says. She's looking at me real funny, like she's trying to see something behind my eyes.

"She's a witch," I hiss. "She was messing Daddy up."

"She was *fixing* him," Tillie snaps. "You don't know anything. You're just mean."

She's not wrong. Inside me, the mean streak turns double edged and sharp as an arrowhead. It twists and turns and hurts until I let part of it out. I used to wonder where it came from, when the rest of my family is so good it makes my teeth ache. Maybe it was born inside me, maybe it was because someone took my momma away before I knew her. All I know is I feel better when I get the meanness out, same way a teakettle's gotta release steam when it gets too hot.

Daddy comes back inside. His eyes are wet and red. "Go to your room, Winnie," he says.

The men arrive with their boots thudding on our floor. Jasper's daddy apologizes.

"Sorry to come like this," he says to Daddy. "My boy here—" his hand drops to Jasper's shoulder, standing beside him, "— says your girl Winnie told him a witch came and laid a spell on you, to hole up here."

"She's a damn liar," Tillie interrupts.

Jasper's been looking around the room, but his eyes snap back to Tillie. "She wasn't lying," he says. "I know. She made me swear you wouldn't hurt her daddy. She meant it."

"We've been having a bit of difficulty with Winnie recently," Daddy says real soft to Jasper's daddy. "Losing her mother so young, you understand. I haven't been home as much, as of late, and I think perhaps maybe she was a little mad at me and this was just her acting out."

My jaw clenches up tight. The muscles in my face tremble. I'm mad, but it still cuts me up, to hear him say that. That he'd pick a witch over his own daughter.

"That true, Caro?"

She nods, and Tillie says again, "I told you she was a liar." Her cheeks are flushed and somehow it makes her prettier. I can feel my own face stained red, but my skin is usually chalk white and if I were to look in a mirror, I would not be prettier.

They act like I'm the bad one, but they're the ones lying. They're the ones who harbored a witch. And now everyone will hate me even more, call me a liar, when I didn't do anything wrong. Inside, red hot fire burns in my chest, branches down my arms, my legs, spreads into my fingers and toes. My eyes meet Jasper's.

"She was here," I say. My voice is weak, not strong, but I say it anyway. I only look at Jasper. I need him to see.

I can feel Daddy looking at me. I know that everything between us has changed, that it will never be the same. "Go, to your room now," he says, and his words are clipped off at each end and his voice is full of ice.

Jasper is staring at me like he can burn a hole in me just by thinking about it. I know I can't say anything now. But I will later, when I'm free of Daddy and Tillie and their lies. Jasper and everybody else have always been right about the witches. We have to get rid of them all. I see Jasper's got a mean streak just like me. Together, we can hang them all and then burn them to bits of bone and ash so they can't come back.

I don't need Daddy or Caro or Tillie, or anyone at all.

I go back to my silent cold room and feel the meanness inside me. It sets its teeth into my heart and pulls at the ragged strip carved through the center. It crawls inside and begins to nest. I think about Milla and how wicked she was. She didn't use real magic, but she cast a spell over Daddy all the same. She was rotten right down to the core. She'll be the first witch to hang. I can hear the chanting in the back of my head. Burn the witch. Hang the witch.

Soon.

See L'Erin Ogle's story "Mean Streak" online at Metaphorosis.
If you liked it, leave a comment. Authors love that!
Remember to subscribe to our e-mail updates so you'll know when new stories are posted.

About the story

"Mean Streak" started when I tried to understand where hatred of a group of people different from someone came from. I have known intelligent, otherwise kind people I have stepped away from due to their opinions and beliefs about who counts as a person in the world today. Winnie, the main character, crept in my head and never left. Winnie hasn't had it entirely easy, her mother died before she knew her, her half sister is prettier and well-liked, and Winnie has the mean streak running though her to boot. Was the mean streak there first? Or did the loss of her mother and the isolation she felt in her remaining family create a wound that scarred into meanness as a way to survive? If Milla hadn't come, would Winnie have wanted to turn to hunting witches? I'll let you decide, but ultimately this story was about discovering where hatred comes from, and if it can be understood. I wrote an ending that didn't fit, because I wanted Milla and Winnie's father to have a happy ending, but it refused to fit into the story. Mean Streak was the first story I've written where some of the narrated passages disturbed me so deeply I felt at odds with writing it — but Winnie was who she was and she had to be written that way.

A question for the author

Q: What is the scariest or most disturbing story you've ever read?

A: I read a short story by Sunny Moraine in *Shimmer* titled "Come My Love and I'll Tell You a Tale." It's narrated by someone grieving the end of the world and their lover. What shook me to the core was the beautiful prose describing the life before, then shifting to the events that ended the world as it was known, to the narrator now. I won't ruin the story for anyone, but the way the narrator was forced to adapt, the things that had to be done to survive, and the knowledge of before and after, the splitting of the soul, never quite left my head or my heart.

And for a novel, Mark Z Danielewski's *House of Leaves* broke my heart, turned me into an insomniac listening for the shift of a house at night, and wrote about regret, heartbreak, loss, and an evil that wasn't defeated. There is a page where the words "I'm sorry" are written spiraling out of control, into an event, that I will never forget. It's an experience, to read that book. It never left me either.

About the author

L'Erin writes speculative fiction from Lawrence, KS aka LFK. She works full time as an ER nurse to pay the bills while raising the human version of Rainbow Dash. She loves all dark fiction and rarely writes happy endings, but is excited about them in real life. In her free time, she's probably watching apocalypse movies, reading dark fantasy stories, and eating cake. Previous works are listed at lerinogle.com

@lerinjo

Copyright

Copyright 2019, Metaphorosis Publishing

Cover art © 2018 by Saleha Chowdhury
salehachowdhury.com

"The Lightkeeper's Wife" © 2019, Amelia Dee Mueller

"The Soul Farmer's Daughters" © 2019, Kyle Kirrin

"The Bear Wife" © 2019, Catherine George

"Mean Streak" © 2019, L'Erin Ogle

Authors also retain copyrights to all other material in the anthology.

Metaphorosis Publishing

Metaphorosis offers beautifully written science fiction and fantasy. Our projects include:

Metaphorosis Magazine

Metaphorosis, a weekly magazine of SFF short stories, including stories from all the authors in this anthology. Find out more at magazine.metaphorosis.com, and sign up to be notified of new stories.

Metaphorosis Books

Recent books from Metaphorosis can be found at <u>books.metaphorosis.com</u>, and include:

**Metaphorosis
2017**

**Metaphorosis
2016**

All the stories from *Metaphorosis* magazine's second year.

Almost all the stories from *Metaphorosis* magazine's first year.

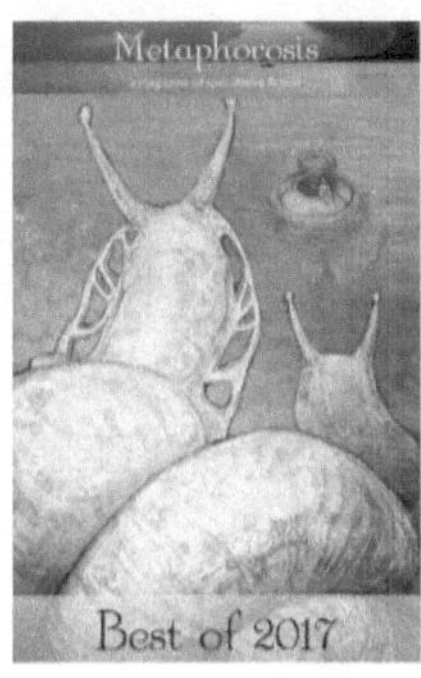

Metaphorosis:
Best of 2017

The best science fiction and fantasy stories from *Metaphorosis'* 2nd year.

Metaphorosis:
Best of 2016

The best science fiction and fantasy stories from *Metaphorosis'* 1st year.

Reading 5X5

Reading 5X5

Five stories, five times

Writers' Edition

Twenty-five SFF authors, five base stories, five versions of each – see how different writers take on the same material.

All the stories from the regular, readers' edition, plus two extra stories, the story seed, and authors' notes.

Best Vegan SFF of 2017

The best vegan science fiction and fantasy stories of 2017!

Best Vegan SFF of 2016

The best vegan science fiction and fantasy stories of 2016!

Susurrus

A darkly romantic story of magic, love, and suffering.

www.ingramcontent.com/pod-product-compliance
Lightning Source LLC
Chambersburg PA
CBHW030210130726
47898CB00012B/964